WORD GIRL

CITY HALL SANDWICH

Adapted by Annie Auerbach

SCHOLASTIC INC.

New York   Toronto   London   Auckland   Sydney
Mexico City   New Delhi   Hong Kong   Buenos Aires

ISBN-13: 978-0-545-10071-7
ISBN-10: 0-545-10071-2

12 11 10 9 8 7 6 5 4 3 2 1   8 9 10 11/0

Designed by Angela Jun
Printed in the U.S.A.
First printing, September 2008

Hi! I'm WordGirl.

Captain Huggy Face and I are from the planet Lexicon.

We crash-landed on Earth when I was a baby.

Everyone here knows us as Becky Botsford and Bob.

But secretly, I use my superstrength and word power to fight evil villains.

Word up!

Becky's mom, Mrs. Botsford, worked at City Hall.

Today she was having a bake sale.

Becky was helping her.

A giant sandwich press appeared over the building!

Uh-oh. Looks like trouble, Becky thought.

She changed into her WordGirl costume and flew into the sky.

"Word up!"

A voice boomed from the machine. "It's me, Chuck the Evil Sandwich-Making Guy. Unless you meet my demands, City Hall is, uh, what's the word?"

"Doomed!" said WordGirl. "But not if I can help it."

"WordGirl!" said Chuck.

But he wasn't afraid.

"When the timer gets down to zero, my sandwich press will crush City Hall!" he said.

"There must be a way to stop it," said
WordGirl.
Chuck nodded. "There is a secret code.
But you will never guess what it is."

WordGirl had to save City Hall!
She tried to push the machine away.
But it was too heavy.

Chuck laughed. "City Hall is, uh, what was the word again?"

"Doomed," said WordGirl.

"Doomed means something bad, right?" he asked.

WordGirl nodded. "It means something that's going to end in disaster."

"Meet my demands," said Chuck.
"Or City Hall is doomed!"

"What demands?" asked WordGirl.

Chuck hadn't thought of any.

"Why don't you go for a walk and think about it?" said WordGirl.

She had a plan. . . .

She sat at the computer and tried to crack the secret code.

"Sandwich? Bread? Meatball?"

But the timer kept counting down.

Uh-oh!

"Maybe there's a file on Chuck in City Hall," WordGirl said to Huggy.

"I'll stay here. You go with my mom to get that file!"

The giant sandwich press moved down with a scary *CLUNK*!

"Go, Huggy! Dash!" cried WordGirl.
Huggy didn't understand.
"You know, *dash*. It means to hurry,
move quickly," said WordGirl.
Huggy dashed away.

WordGirl kept guessing the code.
"Ketchup? Grilled cheese? Turkey?"
But none of them worked.
She could not break the code.

Then Chuck came back.

"I finally know what I want as a demand," he said.

"I want a foot-long sandwich. Take that!"

WordGirl was surprised.

"Really?" she asked. "That's all you want?"

"Well, I don't want to be greedy," Chuck said.

"Isn't that the whole point of this?" WordGirl asked.

"I shouldn't be helping you," said WordGirl. "But try to think of something you have always wanted."

Chuck left to think about it.

He came back a little while later.
He saw WordGirl at the computer.
She was still trying to guess the password.
That made him really angry.
"I'm going to crush City Hall *right now*!" he
shouted.

WordGirl stood up.
"You're not getting past me!" she said.

"I don't have to," Chuck said. *"Ta-dah!"*
He pulled out a remote control.
He pushed the green button.
The timer began to go even faster!

Just then Mrs. Botsford and Huggy showed up.

Huggy had Chuck's file.

"You're not supposed to have that!" said Chuck. He ran after Huggy.

The file flew in the air.

EXIT

Mrs. Botsford picked up one of the sheets of paper.

She read it out loud.

"Chuck's first pet was a little bunny named Fluffy."

"*Noooo!*" yelled Chuck.

There was only one second left!
WordGirl typed F-L-U-F-F-Y into the computer.
It worked!
The timer stopped.

WordGirl smiled at Chuck.

"It looks like the only demands you will be able to make will be in prison!" she said.

A policeman took Chuck away.

And so City Hall was saved from doom by the swift thinking of WordGirl and Captain Huggy Face!

Hello! I'm Beau Handsome and here are today's puzzles.

Let's begin with a "wordoko" puzzle. Fill in the grids below so that every row, column, and box contains the letters named under the board. The diagonal will spell out a word!

d			a
h			
	h		
s		a	

letters: shda

	r		o
d			
			w
	w	o	

letters: drow

26

Read the clues to the crossword puzzle and write the correct word in the squares.

Down
2) A machine that has a screen and a keyboard
3) The name of Chuck's pet bunny
4) The word that Chuck can't seem to remember
6) I wish I _____ fly

Across
1) Chuck's head is shaped like one of these
5) This is WordGirl's favorite saying
7) Captain Huggy Face is one of these
8) WordGirl's parents know her as _____

Find the words hidden in the word search puzzle. Check across, up and down, or diagonally.

S W C R F I L E S Y
E A O T D A S H A R
C S D R B M M C N E
R H E B D C U U D G
E D C I T Y S I W F
T A R E M O T E I L
R H J A R P A F C U
D O O M E D R C H F
B I A R O U D D M F
D E M A N D S R Y Y

mustard
secret
file
word
remote
dash

doomed
fluffy
sandwich
code
demands
city

Unscramble the words below. To give you a little help, each word is listed in the box below.

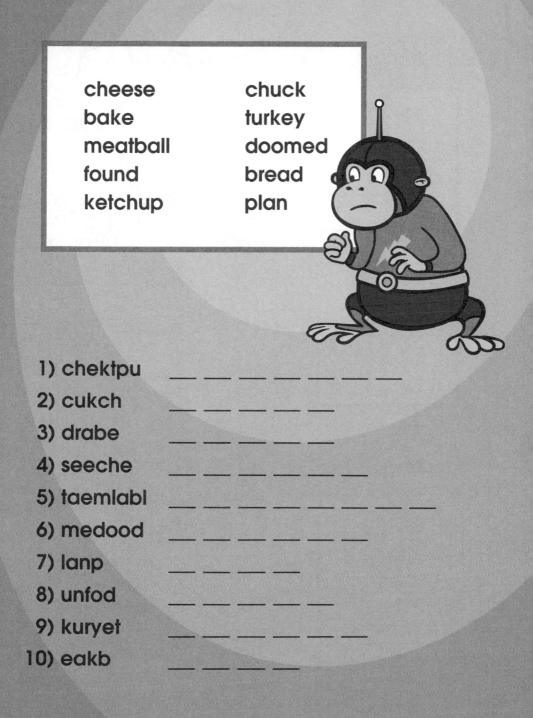

cheese	chuck
bake	turkey
meatball	doomed
found	bread
ketchup	plan

1) chektpu ___ ___ ___ ___ ___ ___ ___

2) cukch ___ ___ ___ ___ ___

3) drabe ___ ___ ___ ___ ___

4) seeche ___ ___ ___ ___ ___ ___

5) taemlabl ___ ___ ___ ___ ___ ___ ___ ___

6) medood ___ ___ ___ ___ ___ ___

7) lanp ___ ___ ___ ___

8) unfod ___ ___ ___ ___ ___

9) kuryet ___ ___ ___ ___ ___ ___

10) eakb ___ ___ ___ ___

Answer Key

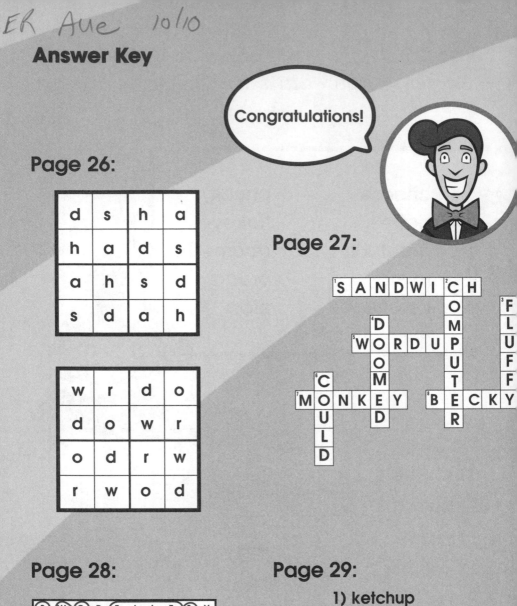

Congratulations!

Page 26:

d	s	h	a
h	a	d	s
a	h	s	d
s	d	a	h

w	r	d	o
d	o	w	r
o	d	r	w
r	w	o	d

Page 27:

Crossword answers:
1) SANDWICH
2) COMPUTER
3) FLUFFY
4) DOOMED
5) WORDUP
6) COULD
7) MONKEY
8) BECKY

Page 28:

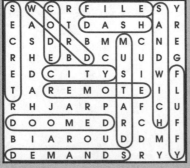

Page 29:

1) ketchup
2) chuck
3) bread
4) cheese
5) meatball
6) doomed
7) plan
8) found
9) turkey
10) bake